MARGRET & H.A.REY'S
Curious George
in the Big City

Illustrated in the style of H. A. Rey by Martha Weston

Houghton Mifflin Company Boston

Copyright © 2001 by Houghton Mifflin Company

Curious George® is a registered trademark of Houghton Mifflin Company.

All rights reserved. For information about permission to reproduce selections from
this book, write to Permissions, Houghton Mifflin Company, 215 Park Avenue South,
New York, New York 10003.

www.houghtonmifflinbooks.com

The text of this book is set in 17-pt. Adobe Garamond.
The illustrations are watercolor and charcoal pencil, reproduced in full color.

Library of Congress Cataloging-in-Publication Data

Curious George in the big city / illustrated in the style of H. A. Rey by Martha Weston.
p. cm.
Based on the original character by Margret and H. A. Rey.
Summary: When they go to the city to see the sights, Curious George gets separated
from his friend and has many adventures before they are reunited.
RNF ISBN 0-618-15252-0 PAP ISBN 0-618-15240-7
[1. Monkeys — Fiction. 2. City and town life — Fiction.] I. Weston, Martha, ill. II. Title.
PZ7.R33 Cui 2001
[E]—dc21   2001024115

Printed in Singapore

TWP   18 17 16 15 14 13 12 11 10
4500286703

This is George.

He lived with his friend the man with the yellow hat. He was a good little monkey and always very curious.

Today George was in the big city.

"Let's stop here, George," his friend suggested. "I would like to get you a holiday surprise before we see the sights."

George loved surprises. He wanted to get a surprise for the man with the yellow hat, too. Why, here was a whole pile of surprises—all ready to go! Would one of these be right for his friend?

George was curious.

He opened a box and peeked inside. The box was empty. (That was not a good surprise!) George opened another box, and another. They were all empty!

Suddenly the store clerk came running. "Stop! Please!" he cried. "You are ruining my display!"

But George did not want to stop. He wanted to go. He wanted to get away — fast! Quickly, he climbed on the escalator. George went up. The clerk went up, too.

What George wanted now was to find his friend. What luck! George spotted a yellow hat on the escalator going down. Could that be his friend?

George wanted to find out.
Soon he was going down, too.

George followed the yellow hat out of the store and around the corner.

He chased it down some stairs. Where could his friend be going? Was this George's surprise?

No, this was the subway!

George got on the train just in time. He thought maybe his friend was playing a game with him. But where was the man now? George looked around. The train was very crowded. Could that be him on the other end of the subway car? It might be hard to get there…

but not too hard for a little monkey!

　　Suddenly the train stopped — and when the doors opened, the yellow hat disappeared. George followed as quickly as he could, but he was too late. This was not a surprise after all. This was a mistake. The yellow hat was nowhere to be seen. Poor George. He was all alone in the big city. How would he ever find his friend now?

Soon George could see nothing but legs. He was surrounded by a crowd of moving people, and he had to keep moving himself so that he would not get stepped on.

Then George heard a woman's voice coming from the head of the crowd. "Going up," she said.

Up! That was just what George needed. He needed to be high
up, like in a tree or on the escalator. Then he could get a good
look around. George joined the crowd as they got into an elevator
and went up.

Here was a good lookout! From up here George could see a bridge, lots of tall buildings, and a little green lady standing in the water. But he did not see his friend.

"It's time to go," called the woman from the elevator. "We have lots more to see." The crowd followed the woman. They wanted to see more. George wanted to see more, too.

Soon George was on a big bus driving through the city.

There *was* lots more to see!

But no matter where George looked,

he did not see the man with the yellow hat.

Back on the bus, George looked and looked. Finally, he saw something familiar. George was excited. He rushed inside. He was sure to find his friend here! Instead, he ran right into the clerk.

"You're just the one I've been looking for to help me fix this mess," he said.

George felt bad. He had not meant to make such a mess.

Could he help rewrap the boxes? George took some ribbon in one hand, some paper in another, and some tape in a third.

Then, like only a monkey can, George wrapped those boxes.
Soon, a crowd gathered to watch. Everyone wanted George to
wrap their boxes, too.

Just as George tied his twenty-fifth quadruple bow, he spotted his friend. At last! George was happy. But when he saw that the man was carrying a present, George became sad. He had forgotten all about finding a surprise for his friend. Then he had an idea...

"George!" exclaimed the man with the yellow hat. "What a good surprise!" His friend was very glad to see him. "I've been looking all over the store for you," he said. "And now I have a surprise for you, too."

George opened his surprise
and put it on.
It fit perfectly.
"Now we're ready to see the
sights," the man said.

George held tightly to
his friend's hand and
everyone waved goodbye.
"Let's be careful not to
get separated again," the
man with the yellow hat
said as they left the store.

"The best part of the holidays is spending time together."
George agreed.

The end.